Toddlersaurus
Time to Eat

Words & Pictures Stuart Trotter

"Hello. My name is **Steggy**...

...and it's time to eat."

Mountains tumble,
what's that rumble?

It's **Steggy's** tummy – hear it grumble!

Open-mouthed, snapping, hopping...

When the ground shakes and quakes...

...it's **Steggy** crunchin

'Gurgle, gurgle, gulp and slurp!'...

First published in 2020 by © Rockpool Children's Books Ltd.

This edition published in 2020
by Rockpool Children's Books Ltd.
in association with Albury Books.
Albury Court, Albury, Thame
OX9 2LP, United Kingdom

Printed in Turkey

ISBN 978-1-912061-76-1 (Paperback)

rockpool
children's books
Albury Books